SOUTHERN SAINTS

ALLISTER NELSON

SOUTHERN SAINTS

Southern Saints

Allister Nelsom

THE LAUGHING MAN HOUSE PUBLISHING

This book is a work of fiction. References to real people, events, establishments, organizations, or locales are intended only to provide a sense of authenticity, and are used to advance the fictional narrative. All other characters, and all incidents and dialogue, are drawn from the author's imagination and are not to be construed as real.

SOUTHERN SAINTS

www.lmhpub.com

Cover Design by Mitch Green

Edited by Janus

Royalty-Free images sourced by Pixabay

For the old gods of Appalachia
And for Josh, my muse.

The Annunciation of
Appalachia Mary

God comes hungry to your table. The crops have rotted. Tins of bean, ash in the cornbread. He asks you for food.

"Mary, only what you can spare."

He comes to talk with you often, driving an old Harley, ramping in with the rains.

It is storm season, and He always washes the dirt away to the roots.

"I did what I could, God."

"I did what I could."

To love God, is self-harm, a Big Thing encased in the cocoon of your thighs.

Afterwards, you wonder at the clear skies, when they had been thunder at His climax.

He smokes Chestertons, and reads Woolf.

"My favorite writer, you know. Second only to you, Mary."

"I can't hold a candle to Virginia, God."

He comes more frequently, when the winter draws, and your camellias bloom.

Snow, in the yard, on your old shit-colored truck.

His Harley crowds the garage.

"Will you be my Bride, Mary?"

"I'm not going to be a pregnant teen like my own, ma, God. Wait a few years."

He does.

When you are twenty-one, God takes you on His usual Harley ride. The storm chases you both.

He brings you up to a cloud, soft on your belly. He lays you down, spends His seed on your feet.

Bathes you in a River. He says it is sacred.

You are not much of one to marvel at sacred things. All the fruits and bread He offers, the wine. It tastes barren.

So you stick to the depot produce when your victory garden fails. The Boys are fighting a War, over There. Joseph left and died in some goddamn field in France.

God always tells you He can bring Joseph back from the Dead, if you want.

"Why disrupt Azrael. He's a kind boy."

"Mary, you are too humble. I'd move Heaven and Earth for you. Why won't you be my helpmate, my Rib?"

"I want to work as a riveter, honey."

So you do. Rosie. Wings on biplanes. Then, you start flying cargo for the Air Force, supplies Stateside for the Boys. Gabriel begs to be copilot, in his soldier uniform, and plays at

War.

"You're twenty-three, Mary. I can give you a Kingdom of Eternity," God whispers between your neck and shoulder, as you picnic in the Shenandoah FDR's boys built. Chestnuts. You remember cracking the meat open in your youth for Christmas, when the woods thinned of deer, and your no-good Papa would show up Christmas Eve, boozy from the mines, with a too-small buck.

Mama cooked it up anyway, they quarrelled, and you prayed

The Rosary.

"I just want my garden to grow, God. You need to be gentler with your Harley. It rains here, so much, even for the Smokies."

The War ends. They find Joseph's remains. God helps you bury him in a plot, in your front yard.

It's the finality, of Joseph – your middle school sweetheart – just bones now.

"I'll be yours, God. But you need a factory job. The Ford factory, or the mines. Make a proper Man of yourself."

So now God comes home, smothered in coal, smelling of salt pork, and your belly rounds with the Moon. Son of Man, Child of Mary.

Heir of the Heavens.

Mortal-born.

When you give birth, you do a home ritual. You read about it in a baby book. Lailah, the angel of childbirth, delivers. You hold Joshua

Bethel in your hands – first of his name, your own nom de plume his last, because God is just God, and Yeshua was too old-fashioned.

You kiss God's brow through your sweat, held on the pounded dirt and hay floor in His strong arms, as Joshua latches.

"What We made is Good, honey," you say.

God and the angels, they sing.

The town loves Joshua. God gentles his rains, turns in the Harley for a dented, used Chevrolet flatbed. You have a Good Life.

And no one dies on a Cross, and you have a daughter. Eva.

God gives it all up in the end, for you. Puts Lucifer in charge. That First Sun repented over the years, Malik Taws you read in a worn dime store copy of National Geographic, a Yazidi girl with dirt cheeks like you and your own green eyes glimmering back from the cover.

She, an Atlantic and then some away, looks like she knows God, knows rains, too.

Good, that. God, Mary, Joshua, Eva.

Normalcy, and He sings you to sleep each night

In His Arms.

And by now, you smoke Virginia Slims, and
you die
    cherished
    In His Arms.
    Joseph greets you at the gate. God stays on
Earth to care for the grandchildren.
    You get a New Beginning, in
    the End.
    "Welcome home, my Merry Little Mary,"
Joseph winks, and you kiss for the first time
in eighty years. Your real true love.
    And that, well?
    That's all you wanted:
    God's blessing, Joseph's kisses for all
eternity.
    Your children Ascend, after they die. God
comes Home.
    And Gabriel still flies copilot as you
shepherd souls in your plane to Gan Eden.
    And all is blooming in your Heavenly
Garden.
    And oh, the rains?
    They come.

Fucked

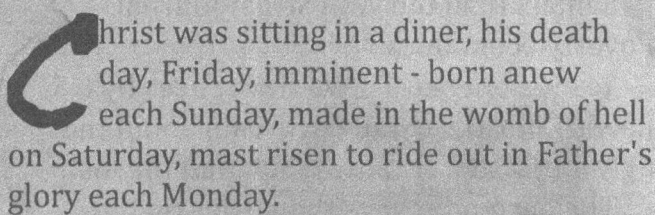

Christ was sitting in a diner, his death day, Friday, imminent - born anew each Sunday, made in the womb of hell on Saturday, mast risen to ride out in Father's glory each Monday.

Sunday was for wine. It was a hipster bar in Richmond, and he poured whiskey and vermouth into a small glass, added honey, and slugged it down, pierced and tattooed with the Shem Ha Mephorash. He played a crusty bass and had sidecuts.

He read the paper, some anarchist zine.

Samael crept up like an old cat. It was a familiar chill. "Michael."

Christ smiled slyly, pulling out his side chair without a look up. "Bartender, vodka on the rocks."

Samael, a black cloud - just some piss ass punk - snaked forwards without the two looking at each other.

Lucifer spiked his drink with Yeshua's soul, the leaves spicing the vodka like fireball whiskey.

They cheered each other up in silence, ice sloshing, and their eyes met - or maybe they didn't, from the Pinnacle to the Pit.

Samael read the Wall Street Journal. Poverty economics.

Yeshua opened Til We Have Faces by C.S. Lewis - mostly just to daydream about the ugly stepsister. He always favored the lost.

The bartender gave them fries on the house.

"How was the week, Mike," Samael finally sighed. "You're lingering." "I started a land war in Asia," Michael sighed, closing his zine. "Never start a land war in Asia."

"Don't quote Princess Bride. It's my schtick." "As you wish."

The ginger and black-haired twins eyed each other up, green eyes on blue, and they broke into laughter.

"Let's go get beers at the Grey Ghost. We can tell Mosby to fuck himself." They slid off the seats, paid in silver tallers, and walked out to Scott's Edition.

Nursing IPAs - Samael a tart, skunky West Coast, Michael a clear New England, they talked. Politics. Heavenly War. Their usual Friday catch up.

As the evening dawned, Jesus began to ache. His bones felt like soil.

And so they walked to Hollywood Cemetery, into the casket church. It was empty, but angels do not need invitations.

Christ and Lucifer laid each other down in a coffin, kissing. First, Lucifer took Jesus's weak body and kissed a line straight down his treasure trail and pink brown nipples to his turgid sex.

Lucifer sucked on Yeshua's olive cock, moaning as he ran incisors of pain and jam down his perineum. He always smelled of baptismal water. It was too holy. So Lucifer bit his vagus nerve, sending dying Christ into ululations of wild Tarzan. Christ came in spurts, white seed and wine erupting from his dick. Lucifer watched idly, lazing about as his brother's eyes began to fade.

"Nice drinking." Michael said, collecting himself. He smiled faintly, then died.

"Nice drinking," Samael sighed, closing the casket, then hauling it onto his back as if it were a brocade.

He made the long journey to Hell, then buried Michael under the rotten apple tree Samael had given up on long ago.

He pulled out the Wall Street Journal and a Marlboro, sipping wine from a flask. It was white wine.

He hated it.

The God of Richmond

Bruisy palms. Lips that cut.
Christ kissed me with wine
        on His Tongue, stained from
fig seed and stem.
I cradled His pierced tongue,
        dirty crust punks in a Richmond
                gutter, we handed out
                        Anarchist zines
went to

                                GWARBar.

I love my God.

God of Rebellion and
mange. The rats flocked
round our ministry, and we

Rambled
with His Rains.

Eve and Lucifer Get Korean BBQ

Eve, Lucifer's fiancée and full-time grad school ornithologist, was grooming Lucifer's wing and doing scientific experiments on the shed feathers as they finished digesting their homecooked fettucine alfredo in their Centreville townhouse. NPR was playing a Prairie Home

Companion reunion with Garrison Keilor and the Wailin' Jennys.

"Yuppie music o'clock, I see," Lucifer sighed languidly, looking like Lestat in a wig. He had dyed his hair blond recently and the bleach was still fresh.

Eve turned it up, squinting at a tailfeather. "You're the folkhead, Lucifer."

The show came to an end, and they settled onto the couch with books. Lucifer read *Infinite Jest*. Eve was re-reading *Gone Girl*. "I think you're a yuppie, Lucifer. The original one. Spoiled young upwardly mobile suburban exile of Hell. With daddy issues."

Lucifer smoked his Juul pod. "Well, I suppose, but my Father only likes Boomer rock, football, and brewskis. I have *much* more discerning taste than G-d."

They flipped on the TV. An old rerun of Gossip Girl was on.

"I don't like Jenny. She's spoiled."

"You're spoiled, Lu. You stole most of the pasta."

"You stole five of my wings."

"For science. I'm making drones that fly on 3D-printed aerial pinions without the need for an engine, with magnetic fields in them like the avian lodestones in your brain. All angels have them, after all."

Lucifer drank Two Buck Chuck. "Huh. Chuck is an asshole."

"You are Chuck."

"You are Blair. Isn't anything better on."

They switched channels. The Good Place was on.

"Chidi is eating a lot of chili-coated Peeps. I feel like that after issuing Executive Perdition to errant Goetic lords in Hell. Drown my sorrows in insanity."

"Do demons have life cycles like Michael? Sadako?"

"I was born perfect."

"Aaah."

Lucifer cuddled Eve and played with her hair. "I wish I was a natural blond," Lucifer sighed. "I was blond before I rebelled. The fall incinerated it black."

"That's not your true form, Lu."

Lucifer shifted into his burnt, sanguine hell skin of horror, pussy, bone-exposed charred corpse form. It smelled like Korean BBQ and made Eve kind of hungry.

"Wanna go get KBBQ. You're hotter like this."

"Monsterfucker."

"Human diddler. You have monkey fever. Your fiancé is a great ape."

"At least you are not a sentient demon corpse."

"Whatever. I want bulgogi."

Eve drove Lucifer to the Iron Age KBBQ by Shilla in Centreville. They ordered a shitton of BBQ, and the meat burning matched Lucifer's shishkabobbed form.

Lucifer distended his snake jaw and exposed his poisonous, flaming void gullet to devour a whole plate full, chewing even the steel chopsticks: "I can regurgitate this from my thorax pouch to save for later. No to-go bags at this restaurant." He pulled out tortillas from Costco and began to wrap kimchi, pickled radish, and pork belly into little tacos.

"Lu, you're supposed just eat them with the sauce."

"I'm the first original thinker, *Calliope*."

"You saw that taco trick on TikTok from a Mexican-American guy who brings torts to KBBQ."

Lucifer simpered. His pus eyes began to weep gore and maggots. Eve picked up a maggot with her chopstick, fried it, then ate it.

"The fuck, Cals."

"I'm trying to understand avian diets. Someday, I'll live on worms, maggots, mealworms and millseed. I'll disappear into the Amazon with the parrots and monkeys and you'll never see me again."

Lucifer ate the rest of the banchan, and they went to go home. "So, you are a birdbrain."

"Only for you, Lu."

And Satan Found the Son of God Comely

I watched Christ idly, threading a snap-ribbon of fine linen my wife Naamah had braided and dyed with infant blood through my fangs.

He whipped himself with goat leathers, this son of god, parched and penitent. It made me ache for my riding crop, to drown my boredom in some stinking whore in Asmodeus' gambling dens. Tempt the Christ, Beelzebub had said. Stinking pig shit. With what? A virgin of the flesh, I had paraded the finest whores of Hell in jewels and oudh before him.

"I will have no Bride but the Shekinah. To mine goes the Goddess," this Christ had said kindly, offering me water turned to wine. It was Alexandrian by the peeling twang of the vine, not unlike mine own vintage I had planted in Baruch.

"And to me go the whores. Say, Yeshua – your friend James brags you walk on water. I would like to see that. Tis a bored matter, tempting an uncorruptible man. Beelzebub is sending me on a busy mission, knowing I'd spend our coffers on beer from Ninkasi and Siduri Brewing Co.."

I handed him a brewski. Christ chugged, then burped.

"The hops on this are earthy, Sam." He smiled that thousand watt, Krishna-universe-mouth smile, like Cain once had in my Chavah's arms. Gone too soon, that.

"You remind me of my first son. A burden too great to bear. Why not give it all over to me, Mr. Christ? I will give you some time off this fucking Savior schtick. Our Father always slaughters his martyrs. Just look at me," I said, pointing to my sanguine rotting flesh, the scarred ridges. "They called me Lucifer, once. I was beautiful."

Christ uncorked another water bottle, turning it to Tuscan white. "I do not think you unbeautiful, Ha Satan."

I picked the wings off a locust then smashed the creature's juices with my toes. I enjoyed hearing it scream. "Oh stop, Son of God. To flattery goes the Devil. That, and opposable thumbs."

"A gift you gave humanity. And they call it Forbidden Fruit."

"How else to wank off? Now that was the gift they run circles around themselves, little brother. *Lust*. Look at Bathsheba."

"I do not envy men or women the sins of the flesh. But I know that, when I look at you, *Sam*, I am tempted to be your salvation."

I curled back, my claws unsheathing, then drew a blade of blood on the Christ's starving cheek. Holy myrrh and moonbeams poured out, burning me. "Do not tempt me to slit your throat, Yesh. The wine and beer are fun and all, but I am here on mission. A parlay, a dance of wit and words."

"And flesh. You made that clear with the friends of my Magdalene. Tell me, Samael, have you ever been tempted?"

I gave it a thought, licking his blood. It tasted of Tyrian murex purple snails. Lilith made a bloody good stew of those when we had Moloch and Tanit over for potlucks. "No. Tempt me with what? I am Prince of Edom, Rome, Air, the World… and Original Sin. Though, as I said, opposable thumbs were a rather useful gift humans muddled in their memories for a poisonous fig. What would you tempt me with, holy boy?"

Christ was a waif, a break-nothing, sow-whit whelp. I could crush him in my wolf jaw in an instant.

"I am thinking of something new. Communion. Salvation. What if the fiery lake my Patmos John will condemn you to—

"Gnarly prophets, damn them—

"Had a failsafe? Lacerate the rib under my heart, Samael. Sup."

My mouth watered. His blood was not just shellfish. There was rain, on my wine grapes and tree. The Star over Bethlehem that had made me weep the first time in ten thousand years.

I dug my fangs into Christ's side. Drank, my poison sinking into him. He sighed, in pain and bliss, and a hunger I had not had since I raped the Shekinah, broke the bitch in my hands so that YHWH would cast his broken bride down to Hell with me (discard Her like He would His Sons, aright) overtook me. Divine fury. I drained him as one Dracula centuries down the line's myth would spring from Samael and Lilith, the original vampires.

Christ, a fragile, broken lotus shell, held up a hand. Blessed me.

"And you are the Son of God," Christ wheezed, blood pooling at his mouth.

I felt His benediction – his benediction, too – slide into my rotten bones.

"Lucifer."

I looked down, my putrid entrails sewing themselves back into now-olive gold skin, proud black curls atop my head again, piercing blue eyes, white wings no longer rot and bone.

I wept. In my anger, I shoved his weak, dessicated form aside.

Christ stumbled to his feet, then, by a power like Moses' staff parting the red sea, stood. His vaginal wound the mystics would commiserate in dank, stuffy British and German taverns over aqua vitae years down the line shone, then healed, I that first being in creation given

The Eucharistic Communion.

"Stand, angel of love, Chamuel, being of beauty. God has heard you, Samuel."

"I want nothing of G-d."

"What if I want you?" he looked on me with amusement. "What if, in the end, I was always the Master you sowed for?"

"Oh fuck Michael, not another parable! Didn't you do enough of those when we were twins, over beers in various dingy Sumerian establishments, during that whole Annunaki-Watcher-Grigori fiasco? Damn Azazel to Hell."

"I think I will incorporate parables into the ministry, elder brother. A kiss, my friend. As of old."

"Before the fairer sex was invented. When all we had were men," I sighed, body whole, I flexed my now-human hand. "You have a way with the Word, Michael-Christ."

We joined, as men, sylvan kisses dancing, then thirst. He was so frail, so small, so holy, in my

hands.

I kissed the Son of God gently.

I felt like I held my life

my wretched soul

in my hands.

"I want a daughter, of our blood, Michael," I wept in his arms afterwards, Christ-Michael having healed after I fed him my zuhama.

"The daughter of Michael and Samael?" Christ mused. "Maybe in 2,000 years, Samael."

"Maybe in

2,000

years."

I kissed him, and we ambled out of the fucking dumbass desert, into Siduri's local chain of Inn Between Worlds Motel.

"I'd make her from our hearts. Name her Liberty."

"The Sorrows of Satan, Crown of Creation, Hope of Hell? I like that." My twin blessed all the wine into whiskey.

"We could make her a writer. Get someone to tell the tragic idles of Michael and Samael."

"Bollocks idea, brother."

"It is odd to hear the Messiah say 'bollocks.'"

"Your proclivity for cussing rubbed off on me after my forty day penance and fasting. Really, Babylonian hookers? You know I only have you, the Magdalene, and Patmos John."

"He is far from Patmos. Decades. And she is qodeshah, unclean."

"Heh, mine own Eisheth. To whores and starborn saqis for lovers, Sam. And brothers, like the Egyptians."

I clinked my glass. Siduri gave us bar peanuts, which I cracked open with my fangs. "More like the Romans, Mike. Incest of emperors and all."

He was so fragile. So tremulous. So pale. I wrapped a covering wing around him to stave off the cold of the ancient bar.

"Communion is a strange idea."

"It's so I can look after them when I'm gone. My flesh, my heart, their blood."

"So you're a vampire, too."

"You taught me, after all, Samael. I learned all my tricks from my elder brother."

"Except the parables."

"We are broken, unworthy creatures, brother," Michael Christ said, leading me out of the bar, out of the end of the sentence, to his flat in Hawaii and art studio on Maui, onto the back of his white crotch rocket, us in biker gear – him white leather, I black, and off we sped

Into eternity.

To Brokenness, I still think, to this day, watching Liberty type in a tiny room in cold Virginia snow.

Odd, the musings
of a demon, no?

The Inelegance of Space

*I*t was not, shall we say, typical of the D.C. suburbs for a healthy-looking, strapping young alien to crash-land his hotrod spaceship on my estate's front lawn.

"Ari, this is private property," I said drily, whiskey on the rocks in hand as I peered out the back porch at my manicured McLean lawn. "It was a hard day on the Hill. I don't know if I'm up to dealing with anymore pointed 'illegal alien' diatribes just because we support Dreamers. Lord knows the Republican media are grueling me, the other Democrats, and of course, my Senator."

Ahriman – hooded gold eyes, tan sandalwood skin, long ringlets of brownish black hair – smelled of attar. As usual, my trespasser was shirtless, fixing his junkyard midlife-crisis ship in some type of reflective metallic blue cyberpunk pants better befitting disco, not an astronaut.

He simply gave me a thumbs up. "Sorry, Carole, just a moment. Not like I had a choice where 'Cygna' landed. Amesha Spenta hit me *right* in the metallic ball sack – of course, metaphorically speaking."

I sipped my whiskey and sighed. "The upkeep here is difficult, and you always hit the bushes. This is a $53 million dollar property that I got in a divorce settlement from the old D.C. football team owner, after all. I need to take an Ibuprofen and go to bed."

Ahriman threw up his hands, then noetically magicked a black leather jacket to appease me, silver lamellar shirt under it. He knew how I felt about youth exposing their midriffs.

The scent of attar and lilies *reeked*. "Sure, Carole. You know this happens sometimes. Your property is right below the warphole of the Pleaides. I never *mean* to crash here, but I appreciate you keeping it a secret. And Carole, dear, you could stand to be, well, a bit more relaxed. You have a stick up your ass tonight."

I eyed his tasteless blue metallic pants. He was carrying a, shall we say, heavy space gun. "Look, Ari. You might be able to solve that."

Ahriman lit a cig. "By what? Writing your Tinder profile last crash didn't reel in many eligible suitors. And the old guy who lived here, whatshisface, *Brad* is more your type. I'm not sure getting a master of arcane sciences, laser guns, and alien machinery to write a Capital staffer's bachelor bait trawls will capture the right audience of men for you."

"Hmm." I adjusted my pencil skirt. "But you got me so many dates last time, dear. And Ari, couldn't you magick a new dress for me, in return for destroying my favorite rhododendrons?" I curled my upper lip, disappointed as thoughts of my last dalliance with a man salted my memory.

"A dress? I could, sure," Ahriman smiled, relenting. We were old acquaintances, after all.

I smiled serenely. "The last one I wore to the First Lady's dog birthday cocktail was *fabulous*, and I met this really great guy in it. Too bad he had the yacht accident in Old Town."

Ahriman jerry-rigged his space cruiser to an impromptu loading dock he had build by my azaleas a few months ago. Eyesore, it was, all silver and lasers. "How old are you, Carole?"

"52 and fancy. But don't tell the boys that. I like to pretend I'm 43. That's what the Botox and facelift is for. I like to keep my face airtight, like a cruiser."

"You are eternally a maiden to me, Carole – incapable of sentient thought, more Procrustean ooze. You know, my dear old hostess, I think you'd do better with a man your age, old friend." He magicked a Corona from my fridge, spaceship engine jetting blue halonic fuel.

"Hmm, well, you see, Ari I like young men. They don't have the gray tendrils of death and anger in them. Millennials and Gen Zer's come with less baggage."

Ahriman leaned against the hood of his ship, his skintight suit reeling up to reveal dusky abs. I couldn't help but imagine – no, Carole. Don't let the menopause heat get to you!

Ahriman spoke languidly, pleased as pudding with himself: "Hmm, well, I'm older than the Big Bang, so I get it. I too delight in tender young things like Jahi the Space Whore, my wife. But to me, dear Carole, you are not even cellular. Just RNA floating in a celestial vat, a speck of nothing. Not even sentient yet. I couldn't even call you spawn. Fleshy waterbag, maybe. And that's only out of *respect*."

"Thanks Ari, you always have a way with words. It's nice you think I'm still young... wish *Brad* had felt the same way before he banged the Washington Commander's cheer squad and his secretarial staff." I turned on the inviting porch light and opened the glass sliding door. "Hey, come inside, Ari - you can at least *look* over my dating profile. Say if the new haircut I got in my profile pic is okay. If my joke answers and "Ideal Date" section gives younger gentlemen any sparks. I just don't know what to write about myself these days..."

"Huh. You need my help? I'm flattered..." Ahriman magicked away the Corona, licked his bottom lip, and stretched like a desert cat, his gold eyes shimmering. "Hmm, well, Amesha Spenta is reconvening on Planet Nibiru right now with the Rebel Federation, so I guess I have time to kill. My meeting with my brother Aeshma Daeva and my wife, Jahi the Space Whore, isn't for another warp hour."

Ahriman and I found ourselves eating a garden salad, fresh from my *own* garden, with a new recipe for dill sauce we tried out. He made it for me from scratch as I soaked my callused heels in some Epsom salts and warm water – walking from the Capitol South metro station to the office and all over Capitol "Hell's" stomping grounds in dress

code-required high heels was a *surefire* way
to get sore feet, and misaligned toes.

Ahriman rubbed my feet, then fed me
some salad with a silver fork. He was doting
on me – oh, the darling youth! Though...
supposedly *I* was the young one here,
considering he was an alien warlord.

"It's good, your produce and my salad
craftsmanship" Ahriman said as he cleaned
up our plates and massaged my back. "Okay,
alright, Carole. I'll write the profile again."

Afterwards, we kissed, made love as usual,
and tended to our own inner gardens.

*A*hriman's profile had worked, for a bit.
He had written some Persian whirling
dervish poetry – Rumi, he said, whoever
that was – rehashes, to make me sound like I
read love poetry and was literate beyond
legal files. Then, Ari had finagled my favorite
ice cream flavor – pistachio – into a quip

about men's dress shoes, and how I'd like to kiss a man with his shoes *off*.

Ahriman met me for coffee at Northside Social on Tuesday after we worked all day – me on the latest Senatorial bill, him on his spaceship clunker

Ahriman stirred his cappuccino, pensive, gold eyes hooded with malaise: "So, how'd the latest string go, Carole? And is Brad giving you shit? My ship is in the shitter."

"Why did you call me, Ari? I told you to never call me. The psionic waves you emit on my iPhone always freezes it. Text next time, *dear*."

"Hmm, well, I tried to fly the ship, right, but the engine gave out – halfway through launch, *fuck me, Carole.* I unfortunately crash-landed in Dyke Marsh. I, uh, need to couch surf again."

"Not my yard this time?"

My sometimes Alien Loverboy winced, then checked his ether watch. "No, the warp to the Pleiades had a dakini maiden army guarding it, and the Peri traders weren't far behind. Amesha Spenta is up my *ass* lately, Carole." Ahriman sipped his coffee, jittery –

the drink black, *black* like his combat boots. A bead of dark liquid clung to his lip, the liquid hot and sinuous. He was shaking. I held his hand, making soothing noises, and squeezed it. Tears of blood formed in his stressed eyes, silvery-indigo, and his eye membranes nictated like a Siamese cat.

I smiled gently: "No couch needed, Ari. You deserve a proper rest. I'll fix up a guest room."

"Thanks, old friend." Ahriman smiled, squeezing my hand back, then gulped down the cappuccino. "Aaah. Say, why don't you have kitchen staff, Carole? Robotic scullery maids? Slaves to roast space ox and spill their vittles to divine the war? Wait, you wage no wars. Except against Republicans. Whatever those are."

"Yes, Ari. Yes. See, I'm private. Brad always fucked the maids."

"**I**t's late, Ari. What are you doing watching TV?"

"Jahi the Space Whore called. She's cheating on me," Ahriman sobbed, his oud-fragrant, oiled curls buried in the pillows, looking like a wounded lion. "I fucking *knew* it."

I swallowed my quip of how Jahi, the Space Whore, always, well, prostituted herself to Amesha Spenta like clockwork on Tuesdays.

"Well at least turn something better on than Anakin Skywalker reruns," I said kindly, my motherly instinct kicking in, though I had never been blessed with little ones of my own –

infertility was a curse, you know, but I liked to mother the youth in my life, and mentor young interns. Ahriman drew out that same maternal streak.

"He's a bit relatable, Carole. This Anakin child. Talented at war. Dark-edged. Set against on all sides. No luck in love."

"Murdering his one and only true love – his wife Padmé?"

"Oh, I'd love too!" Ahriman howled, suddenly slamming my old duct-taped together remote onto the couch and turning into his dragonic lion form, bat-winged with scorpion tail stalking my halls, like I had once seen on a museum exhibition at the Met about Zoroastrianism.

"Fuck women!" the Beast of Ahriman growled.

"Well, good night, try to get some rest. And not *all* women are heartbreakers, Ari."

Done raging, he fell asleep, a pile of claw, scorpion appendages, lion fur, and fangs. His void tentacles writhed, dripping poison onto my midcentury modern sofa.

I plumped the pillow, then dusted Cheeto crumbles off the blanked Ahriman's beast form snoozed fretfully under as I cleaned up his mess. The Corona had spilled some yellow drops of beer, and his lime was half-chewed. "Typical man blues. At least he's faithful, unlike Brad, the absolute *ass*," I sighed, fixing my steel bob in the mirror.

I looked back: a mature, elegant, stunning woman – the doctors made sure the nip-tuck did the base work, and the hairdresser put the final touches on my Capitol Hill armor.

"I'm sure to steal a heart at the First Lady's dog Baptism tomorrow."

I opened today's mail, tired from a long day as Media Officer for the Senator. "Hmm, what's this? Carole Derringer and.. 'plus one' to Baxter the Dog's Baptism? *I need a date*?"

Ahriman looked a bit out of place in the White House, his muscles straining his suit. His predator instinct was triggered at Baxter the dog sniffing his pants, and his Beast of Ahriman claws accidentally appeared, tearing his lapel.

The Senator looked at me with imposing blue eyes. "And Carole, my favorite girl, how did you meet Ari?"

I faked ingenue mannerisms, attempting to blush demurely. The Senator liked shallow, one-bit innocent girls. Unimaginative man. "Oh, us? Hah! A jazz bar." The sound of my overly feminine voice grated my mind, just as my patent leather pink pumps dug into my heels.

Performative femininity? UGH.

"Oh?" The Senator watched Ahriman crouch on the floor with Baxter the baptized dog, stalking him. Ahriman let out a lion's roar: Baxter whimpered and peed. "Well, Gen Z is very interesting. At least this Ari fellow is spirited."

"Yes," I smiled. "I'd like to see where this relationship goes."

Ahriman, triggered by the animal's whimper, ate Baxter.

The Senator whistled low, impressed: "Say, Carole: you think we could hire your boyfriend to do opps?"

I winked at the Senator, twirling a bang – *eugh*. He was gazing at my cleavage. "I'll see, sir, I'll see."

Ahriman stalked, bloody, to the lavender lemonade punch bowl, dunked his Beast of Ahriman head in – half-transformed – and gulped the contents down into his flaming gullet. The crystal container shattered.

The First Lady laughed. "Why, Carole, he's delightful! Just like Brad."

"Hmm, yes, ma'am. You always *did* like Brad."

"A toast!" The First Lady said. "To the young, handsome staffer that put Baxter out of his misery! Now that Baxter's baptized – I never got around to it, you know, for sixteen years, the President said my dog was going to Irish Catholic Limbo – I feel my dear old Baxter can pass on properly to Heaven with Catholic Rites."

Ahriman froze. "Cheers? For me? People... really... like me...?"

He sobbed, then bowed.

"Take that you BITCH, Jahi!"

The staffers cheered.

A hriman and I excused ourselves later that evening to Ben's Chili Bowl.

"That party was nice." Ahriman scarfed down a chili-covered hot dog. "Not as good as your cooking, Carole, but it does hit the spot."

"I just don't understand men, Ari," I sighed, blue. "You charm everyone. I can't even keep a man faithful. I'm old, Ari. Too old for love."

Ahriman's eyes grew tender. "Carole, I'm as ancient as Gog and Magog and the Space

Antipodeans. To me, you are not even capable of mitochondrial digestion."

"You have such a way with words, Ari. I wish Earth had true romantics like you." I took his hand in mine. "Say, how is Jahi?"

Ahriman began to sob. "Gone."

"Oh, dear, I'm sorry."

"It's done. I got the divorce from Jahi the Space Whore. Amesha Spenta – my evil twin brother – can have the bitch."

"Welcome to the divorcee club, Ari." I said kindly. "You're a good man, Ari. You'll find someone kind, someone faithful."

He smiled through his tears. "And Carole, so will you."

We walked hand in hand through the autumn spiced rain, and went to go

hear

jazz.

Realizing, finally that we had found each other, happily ever after.

'GENESIS,' speaks-yah

Wine my sacred drink, Baruch and Cana's vine two of the same – like my two Trees, Knowledge and Life.

In the Beginning was the Woman, and in partheogenic Creation, she birthed her lover, Eurynome Eve and Samael Ophion. He wrapped around her, tail fructating Eve's innards, into pregnant cosmic fervor. Those were the times of Great Making, when Snake and Woman danced in tandem – corte to tango, polonaise, mazurka. But he dipped her too far, shattered her starry womb, and out came the Egg of Nekek-Er.

Smatterglass Universe. They cavorted, making love in the slippings. Stars birthed, orgasmic sigh, but all Snake could do was watch Woman Birth, Create, Dream. He wanted to Dream too. So, he, Prometheus-Aion, made Man.

No spirit, in that Creation. Adamah – mud. So he asked his dear Woman – make from my child's rib a soul. Eveling, Norea, Chavah, Lilith, Mary. They had so many children between them, Snake and Woman, but they were bodiless, and Samael's Man would not come alive without the Eternal Soul. So Eve donned Woman, Samael-Michael the Ophite God donned Man, and they lived in the Gaden, for a Time.

Adam-Samael planted the Trees, and Eve tended the Waters. Calamity, clash of Id and Superego, Men are from Mars, Woman from Venus. Fall, from Grace, Adam-Samael saw how his Sons strayed, Daughters he wanted for Himself. The Shekinah – first to exist, last to Kill – argued with Yah the Snake.

The Great Divorce. Heaven and Hell the aftermath. Eve and Samael warred. Eve-Lilith descended to Exiled Earth – cast out of the Serpent's Lapis Exilis breast – to walk with her Fallen Children. And so God lost his Asherah, and Samael lost his Bride.

Ride the Serpent, women still do, arcing over their husbands. Samael split into Michael and Satan, found sadistic comfort in the biplanar hemispheres of His Bicameral Mind, that great Gevurah severance.

Angels and demons, corrupt. Hell intact.

The Earth without

A Soul.

And we talk of Forbidden Fruits, fallen Watchers and Nephilim, angels having no soul.

But once there was Serpent and Eve, and they Loved, and they Danced.

And on each New Year's Eve, Satan and Chavah meet again, set aside pride

And Waltz

Shekinah Enfolded

In Lucifer's
Light.

Eternal Famine of the Soul

Alabaster skin leaves bloody petals on my dressing board. I take my talons and dredge them through my shining flesh, adamant sparkle against wicked nails, and crimson pours forth.

A snaggle tooth sharp canine, grinning arcanely. I look at my reflection, shedding my snakeskin. First, albino serpent scales, shimmering with moonlight. Then, clandestine wings, littering the immaculate marble floor, shot through with veins of gold.

Eve watches. Eve is always watching, through cycles of time, praying that I can find refuge – fuck my little savior. There is nothing but to be harrowed in Hell, and though I am Prince of her World, Gehenna is fructified only by it's regent's scarred flesh and ichor foliating like seeds deep into the blood-soil.

"Do you like it, little girl?" I sing, slipping out of my skin, fileting myself to bloody ribbons.

She cries, praying. I laugh like a madman, sanguine horror of my body hanging in ruins.

"It doesn't have to be like this, Lu."

She dots her eyes of tears.

I reach out – across paens of time, across seas of evil, and lust rises in my groin. I send myself across the Abyss of my Father to her pale pink room.

"It always has to be like this. There is not truth but justice. And I am a *sinner*, Eve."

She begins to dry my wounds, the caul of my bloody rebirth staining her carpets with gore. Sandalwood incense. A rosary of olive wood from Israel – oh, so my charge has been praying for my supposedly wayward soul.

"I will pay the tithe for you, Lu."

She kisses my brow as I bend into her lap, crying out as she applies poultices. My lower naga half wraps around her, strangling her legs. She winces as I draw my thumb claw across the meat of her thigh, digging in. I ruin her many times, cutting apart, click clack of silver blade, her nubile flesh.

Planting my sons deep in my hellwife's womb.

Oh, we fuck. Of course, we fuck in the ruins of my body. When are Lucifer and Eve not fucking? Samael and Asherah? The Bride and the Whore.

"Nachash," Chavah whispers, losing herself in my husks, a quicksilver flame

to my darklight.

"Yes, Eve?" I eat her out like my favorite parfaits. She is crying, agony and ecstasy – her vagina is my favorite place to burrow, tongue laden with her honey, her delicate sweet folds hot and wet under my thumb.

"Do you love me? Do you love anyone? Are you even capable of love?"

"Like a mother albatross's blood from her heart, to feed her children."

I spear into her, laying her down in sweet ruin. My white feathers rain down on her golden breast like marabou. Her blonde hair and blue-green eyes are misty. She begs for kisses. I, of course, oblige.

"Will you leave me, one day, Lu? Never to return? Even when your whole being is lost in me, I can feel the eternal famine of your soul."

"A Beast is hungry, Eve."

"Through eternity?"

"Always, Eve."

"Always."

A Toast to All Our Hells

There's little mystery left to men in this day and age. From factoryworkers to salarymen, they sit either in assembly lines or tinker in dinky offices, thirsting after long forgotten days of carnage, war, and glory in video games and Gloria Et Romana. The grey ghosts of this world bury their masculine Ids six feet under where my husband Samael lives.

There isn't much left in this world to intrigue an ancient goddess. Lilith, they call me, killer of infant souls. Queen of Hell, Nightmare Raven, Seed-Stealer and Seductress. Yet men have their little kinks I find intriguing, tiny cracks in the modern Ubermensch that display the inner animal – and women, beneath their painted cheeks and milquetoast vanilla note perfumes, can be even more vicious and unhinged.

Oh, how I love the sons of Adam and daughters of Eve. I was there when Rome burned, fiddling Nero off in his marble bathtub. I came to Joan of Arc in her prison, promised her a happy place in my military after *dear* old Michael had abandoned his protégé to the stake. I picked Jezebel's remains from dog's teeth and gave her a proper burial, wept with Bathsheba and raged with her the night her husband was killed and David raped her – bastards always, those unfallen Sons of God.

I mourned with the Marys. I am the Shekinah's handmaiden, after all, and I serve Sophia in my own ways – *Iesu* was her most loved child. All I am is an afterthought, a

cautionary fable turned feminist icon. I
plotted with my old lover Chava to liberate
our daughters, and we poked Marie Curie
and Margaret Sanger enough to invent
modern science and birth control, worked up
the Brontes and Austen into inventing the
Gothic and romance novel, inspired Rosa not
to give up her seat (but thanks, dear. for the
poisoned offer), and above all - *we raged*.
Chava and I raged. We still rage.

It's been a long day. Countless women and
children murdered. Samael brings home the
dead, laboring always in reverse birth pangs
as the Reaper, and Eve and I tend their souls,
helping them pass on with the aid of Gabriel,
Lailah, and Dumah. I needed a break. I
needed a bar.

So here I am, New York City on Christmas
Eve, a Jewish girl with no reason to celebrate
(Samael has spoiled me at Hanukah), and I
am in a little black slip of nothing and faux
minx fur muff (murdering animals is
something I could never do. Children either,
for the matter – the older rabbis always got
my story wrong. Mine was a story of what
women were *owed*, not what we *stole*), with a

Tisch ballerina at my side. Her name is Raquel.

We share drinks. Toast the night. Kiss – her lips are like cherries – and I take her back to my palatial penthouse that towers in a razor-thin metal needle above Central Park. I lay Raquel down on a bed of black silk and white roses, and with my tongue, sex, and fingers, I spoil my little dancer rotten.

The church bells toll for Christmas. The arrival of a Savior I care not a whit for – I still wait for some fabled Messiah to come. Then, the Shekinah can ascend, freed from her perpetual sleep, and I and my sisters Agrath, Eisheth, and Naamah will be made into the Horae again, and Samael shall lose the poisonous Mem from his name – *Samael turned to Sa'el* – and become one of Heaven's most shining covenants.

For now, I smoke a Virginia Slim as snow falls over the Hudson. Raquel is lounging in bed, drinking hot cocoa. Her blonde hair reminds me of my lover Chava. But her breasts are too tiny and pearled to bear the First Mother's burden. I am the Last Mother, Birther of Monsters (though Chava labored

with many of Samael's own in her exile from
Adam, and now Adam prefers the gold stones
of sterile Heaven to any rich roses of Hell)
and I?

—am left to carry on, picking girls piece by
piece up after honor killings, wiping away
tears after acid attacks, mending wombs and
baby bones back together after back alley
abortions forced upon minors by beer-
stinking uncles and cousins.

Chava and I ride the North Wind.

We bring in the forgotten.

We still champion freedom.

And we remember the women.

All of them.

Raquel sighs lightly in her sleep, and I tuck
her gently in, kiss her brow, and smile at this
daughter of Lilith, this daughter of Eve – so
tender are our daughters in their passions, so
kind and loving in their gaze.

It makes a woman proud to be a mother.

I ride the Black Horse, Eve champions the
White Mare.

She brings in the Living, I bring in the
Dead.

Womb and Tomb, the Oak and Ivy, Forever

And Ever
Entwined.

the horror at the center of
the world

*I*t is a story told the worlds round, whispered when one thinks no one is looking.

Lucifer stormed into God's throne room with a fury that roiled the sky. He judged his Father in wrath, mad with the hunger of the abyss he had traded his heart to for wisdom.

The room was empty. God was gone.

Under the ashes of broken sky knelt a girl at the golden throne. She wept, hair long in sorrow. His heart twinged at what he had done, but he swallowed his remorse. In God's throne sat a child. Metatron, his Last Word. Blue-eyed and silent, watching. A silver crown shone on his white hair.

Lucifer moved to slay him.

"No!" the girl cried out. "Haven't you done enough? You would kill a child for vengeance? He is innocent!"

"Eve, you idiot. Do not get in my way!" he said harshly. His eyes were alien to her. Completely swallowed by the void. She was the only one that had seen his madness, when all Heaven was blind to it. Now, he was part of the blackness. He wore a severe robe, sharp like the edge of a blade. There was nothing of the softness she had known.

"Have I taught you nothing?" He raised his sword, eyes keen. He tried to reason with her. "I will restore justice. For my brothers. For our dream. Death is the price of freedom."

"I hate you! All you say are lies. You are a monster."

Lucifer froze. His last shred of humanity flickered, turning his eyes their soft blue. It fled, and the void swallowed it, making them pits. Eve, horrified, could not look away from the light at the end of their tunnels. His voice was raw and ragged, like the arctic wind.

"I am the highest of angels, the most beautiful. What have you become? I am your teacher, your keeper, and you side with the Father? Everything I have done, I have done for you. I love you. Now please, do not interfere."

For the first time in her life, Eve defied him. "You know nothing of love," she spat. The words broke her heart and her laughter. In eons later, Lucifer would wish for it, but hear silence, the sea of darkness locked in his chest cold as death.

In that moment, he was at his wickedest. Desire stripped him to the truth, now a skeleton of razor wit. A crown of thorns twined round his skull.

"You are mine!" he roared in a voice that shook all the heavens, echoing over the falling corpses of angels as his army shredded their souls apart. That sound, wretched, degraded into a cry. It was chaos, something the angels, sweet of music, had never heard. He took her violently, until her legs ran with blood. Her screams mingled with his.

In hunger, Lucifer ripped open his chest, stole the woman's soul, and chained her inside, in black alchemy made her his heart, so that he could live on in the darkness with Heaven's light.

He left a husk of a girl, Eve - now human - after Norea's flight from the raping archangels.

Michael heard it outside the door, saw what Lucifer had done. He has not smiled since. Quietly, Michael picked up the broken woman. Eve bawled her lover's name, her immortality stolen by the harsh black claws of the Nachash's exile.

Lucifer was nowhere to be seen. He left the corpse of a child behind. The crown lay at the infant's feet.

God's Last Word was a question: "Why?"

Michael did not cast his brother out. Lucifer broke the heart of his twin. At the lip of the abyss, he made a choice. It has rippled

waves through time and played like dust on
the minds of poets. Each night since, he has
torn open his chest, skinned himself to
bloody shreds searching for answers.

He has yet to find one.

God of Flies

And the fly, too, is beauty.
God loves all things great,
but moreso, the

small.

Thousands of beetle gems,
the soft breath of dragonfly

wings upon silky river, spiders
milking for their young, the jump
of katydid, and the small

Tenacity

of roach.

E.O. Wilson found G-d
in ants.

And maybe I

find happiness

in death –

the cycles, *perch*, Buzz

of Life.

A Lady's Guide to Courting Archdemons

Emma was sitting at Barnes and Noble, reading *A Court of Thorns and Roses* for the bajillionth time, when she thought she had an aneurysm – that, or was going crazy:

In the 'Interior Design' magazine section, a portal to Hell opened, demon blood thunder sparking in the ozone-smelling shattered reflection of reality. Out stepped a pitch black dragonic demon, covered in tentacles, long black hair, and abyssal red eyes. He was naked, muscled and towering save for a worn brown leather tunica, a burning magma sword sheathed at his hip.

Emma dropped ACOTAR into her latte. "Uh. Uh. Uh."

The dragonic demon browsed an IKEA catalogue, humming to himself, as the Hell portal closed. People walked through him – he invisible and translucent and immaterial to all but Emma.

"The Swedes are geniuses," the demon said, licking his smoldering thumb and turning the catalogue over. He reached into his tunica pocket for his refurbished Blackberry and took a photo of an iced white chair set with a gray steel frame in the catalogue. "This will be perfect for my office."

Emma knew how urban fantasies went: demon shows up only you can see, it means either Jace Weyland is about to arrive – or you, yourself, are the Chosen One.

"Well, no Jace, and my ACOTAR is ruined," Emma muttered, fixing her brown hair back in a messy bun, putting her Dr. Who Tardis

Cat-themed bookbag firmly, quietly down, then snuck up and tackled the demon.

"Fucking shit?" the demon said. Emma ended up not even registering a "clink" on his obsidian flesh. "Was that a flea? Oh, a mortal. Hello, darling."

"Um, that was supposed to hurt you, Mr...?"

"Oh, me? Belial. I guess you have the Second Sight. Scottish by any chance?" He helped her up, surprisingly gentle. He was, actually, quite handsome – for a gigantic muscled half-dragon man.

"Uh, yeah, my nana is Scottish. She was the daughter of a fairy doctor."

Belial smiled a toothy, fanged grin, dusting her sweater shoulder off genially. "Well, it's nice to meet a girl who likes books. All the women in Hell just watch Real Housewives of Gehenna and get virgin blood facials. I don't really like women with a body count."

"Body... count?"

"You know, murdering thousands of nubile Romanian maidens to bathe in their viscera. I'm more into Jane Austen fans. There aren't any in Hell besides Lilith, and she's been married to Samael since they split apart out

of the dregs of wine of the noonday fungus of
Isaac. You know, 'Treatise on the Left
Emanation.'"

"Sure. Well, yeah. I get you. I can't find
anyone into Science Fiction or Fantasy at my
Creative Writing classes. They all read – gag –
litfic."

"Oh god, girl, *fuck* litfic. I'm much more
into Tolkien and Moorcock."

"Wait," Emma paled. "You've read
Moorcock? Elric?

"Hell yeah. And Game of Thrones, House of
the Dragon, Heartstoppers, Wizards of
Earthsea, American Gods –"

"YOU LIKE GAIMAN?"

"Yeah, hey?" Belial softened, then
magicked a human form. He was now only
5'11, tan, sandy blonde hair, gray eyes,
stubble – dressed like a Mudhoney fan.
"What's your name, dear?"

She blushed. "Emma Worthington."

"Say, uh, Emma, wanna get Indian? I know
a joint around the corner. None of the
archdemons really talk books with me but
Lucifer, and he's on a Classics kick lately,

won't shut the bloody fuck up about Jethro's Daughter, Gilead, or Venus in Furs."

"I, uh – yeah, let me pay for my coffee. I'd love that. Can I call you Bel?"

"Yeah, totally. Here, I'll treat you. It's not often I meet another Melnibone fan."

The cashier ringed her up, Belial paying. Belial brushed Emma's arm accidentally while reaching for his bloody AmEx card, then he blushed too.

"So, um… what's your body count, Emma?" Belial asked as they walked to *Hanuman's Delight*.

"Uh… zero?"

"Great, mine's three trillion a year. You know, insurrections, assassinations to quell, beer pong – it gets brutal, down in Hell. I like to let sweat off at Earth."

Emma smiled. "You're not, well, that violent right now. And have good taste in books."

Belial smiled, his brown eyes glimmering like Kentucky whiskey. "So do you, Miss Emma."

They talked Chosen One Syndrome, enemies to lovers, grumpy and sunshine, hurt-comfort, what magic powers they wanted, their favorite sci fi dystopians, and meet cutes.

"This was great Emma, say, can I see you again?" Belial said, standing by the portal to Hell.

"Um, well, I'm actually free tonight, and I kind of want to check out your limited-edition Elric of Melnibone, Bel, so... can I see your library?"

Belial kissed her, spicy and sweet, and she could have died of his lips right there, not minding being another addition to his body count.

"Hell yeah, Emma. I'd love to show you my Warhammer miniatures too. I just got into Age of Sigmar. Fuck it's awesome. Do you like rosé wine?"

Belial scooped Emma up without a second thought in his dragon arms and nuzzled her with his fangs. "Sorry, I'm getting ahead of myself. I tend to go for, uh, cute girls who like my taste in books. I hope I'm not, well, too forward."

"No, Bel. I love Warhammer. I can't wait to see what Henry Cavill does with it. Let's go check out your library."

And that was how a human Booktok girl joined Belial and Asmodeus' Tzeentch army.

The Devil and Two Buck Chuck

"**L**ucifer, can you stop molting? I have to study for my dissertation," Eve said, examining hawk skulls in her makeshift kitchen laboratory as her immortal demon boyfriend was preening.

"I can't help it, *Eveling-*

"THAT'S NOT MY NAME."

Lucifer shot her poison blue irises: "Heh. Well, you see, 'tis my brother Christ's time to be Harrowed in Hell, and I must suffer our wager-

"That's great Lu, but you're late on our half of rent for our townhouse. Grad school TAing doesn't pay well, and you keep ordering Chinese takeout."

"I am paid in blood, Eve." Lucifer strummed his guitar, his lithe, tall, pale form dressed in ripped, faded acid wash jeans, an old black band tee, and combat boots.

"Could you get a job at Trader Joe's, Lu?" Eve looked at him under her fringe of blonde bangs. She said it kindly. "You're kind of a bum."

He harrumphed, strumming a vibrato. "But Beelzebub and I have *band practice*," Lucifer complained, his long, dark black hair a shadowy fringe on his face.

"I'll let you get a hound finally, if you work."

"DEAL."

Lucifer had trouble fitting his bat wings under a peppy Trader Joe's shirt. He grunted, annoyed that his talons kept shredding the Two Buck Chuck he was trying to bag.

"You're such a handsome young teenager, darling," a bespectacled elderly Korean auntie said in dulcet tones, handing him some tacos to bag.

"Thanks, but I'm older than God's Light upon Creation." He smiled seductively. "Say, Jiehon. How about I give your wastrel son a winning lottery ticket to take care of you in your old age in return for your soul?"

"That's okay, little boy. I have a 401k and pension."

Lucifer rang up the tacos. "What is this strange talk? 401k? Pension? I have never heard of such odious languages and portents and omens."

Jiehon patted his clawed hands. "Yes, child, well, they came with being Postmaster. Have a good day, and maybe cut your hair."

"Long hair in hell signals virility."

"Yes, I am sure virility is important to attract girls at your middle school. Here, have this you precious boy. I make them at church." She slipped a jade bead bracelet onto his wrist with a meditation symbol and bell on it, then left, shuffling off with her tacos.

"Perplexing," Lucifer said, turned in his timecard, then mounted his Hellbeast and rode the midnight road of sinners and burning souls back to his townhouse in Centreville.

"Eve, what is a 401k."

Eve looked past pinnate feathers from a dissected, frozen toucan after comparing them. "Oh, you know Lu. Retirement."

Lucifer frowned over cooking ramen. "The woman at Trader Joe's said the strangest thing: the American government not only provides her contributions to her 401k, but a pension."

Eve looked up from her calipers. "Oh, well, so does the Smithsonian and my grad department. It's pretty standard, honey."

"I would think to implement a "401k" and "pension" with my Prime Minister Beelzebub in Hell."

Eve gently set her studies down, then went into the kitchen to chop chives for the ramen. "That's very forward-thinking as Emperor of Hell. I was also very impressed when you stopped torturing souls after I said they could be better put to use at assembly lines for pitchforks."

"Our pitchfork-to-coal-pipeline rate has done well under your auspices, allowing fire imps supplies to keep the fires of Hell burning."

She threw the chopped chives into his pot as he stirred in sauce, then kissed him on his pale neck. He burbled with a moan, then pinned her on the floor, had his way with her as much as she devoured him, right there as usual on the tile.

Just in time, they came for the ramen to almost bubble over. Then, Lucifer and Eve did facemasks, ate mint chocolate chip Ben and Jerry's, and watched Twilight.

What do you mean, a retirement system? You're beginning to sound like an idiot human," Beelzebub mused, laughing as they smoked an apple bong in Eve's garage.

"Pass it, bro," Lucifer said, and Beelzebub withdrew the apple bong from his mandible and strummed his white Gibson, plucking an arpeggio.

They jammed, then discussed retirement. It wasn't long until Penemue approved the new system in his Clerical Department, and Lucifer and Beelzebub couldn't imagine Hell without a guaranteed pension plan for its most valued elderly demon employees.

At the Harrowing of Hell, Christ and Lucifer were playing Mario Kart as they both shed their wings and drank Pilsners in Eve's basement.

"Fuck I hate molting," Jesus said.

"Yeah no shit," Lucifer sighed, rubbing his scales on his wings. "Fuck Rainbow Road."

"Let's do Peach Beach, dude," Jesus said, eating some Cheetos. "Fuck the Harrowing."

Eve wandered in, a kestrel feather in hand, plate of strawberry cake in the other. "Desert, darlings." She handed it to them.

"Thanks, Chavs," Jesus said, saluting her. "Say, you're really humanizing my twin Satan. Seriously. No more torture. A pension system in Hell. Next, he'll become Christian."

Lucifer fingered Jiehon's church-made bracelet, smiling at the cool touch of jade under his talons: "I think I prefer Buddhism, and the faith I find in people working at Trader Joe's."

"It was all him, Yesh." Eve smiled, muttered about bird mating, then left, her glasses askew.

"I kind of like humans, after all," Lucifer admitted. "But I hate Taylor Swift. Eve won't shut the fuck up about her."

"Hell yeah, man. Doom metal all the way." Jesus fist bumped him, and they ate

Strawberry

Cake.

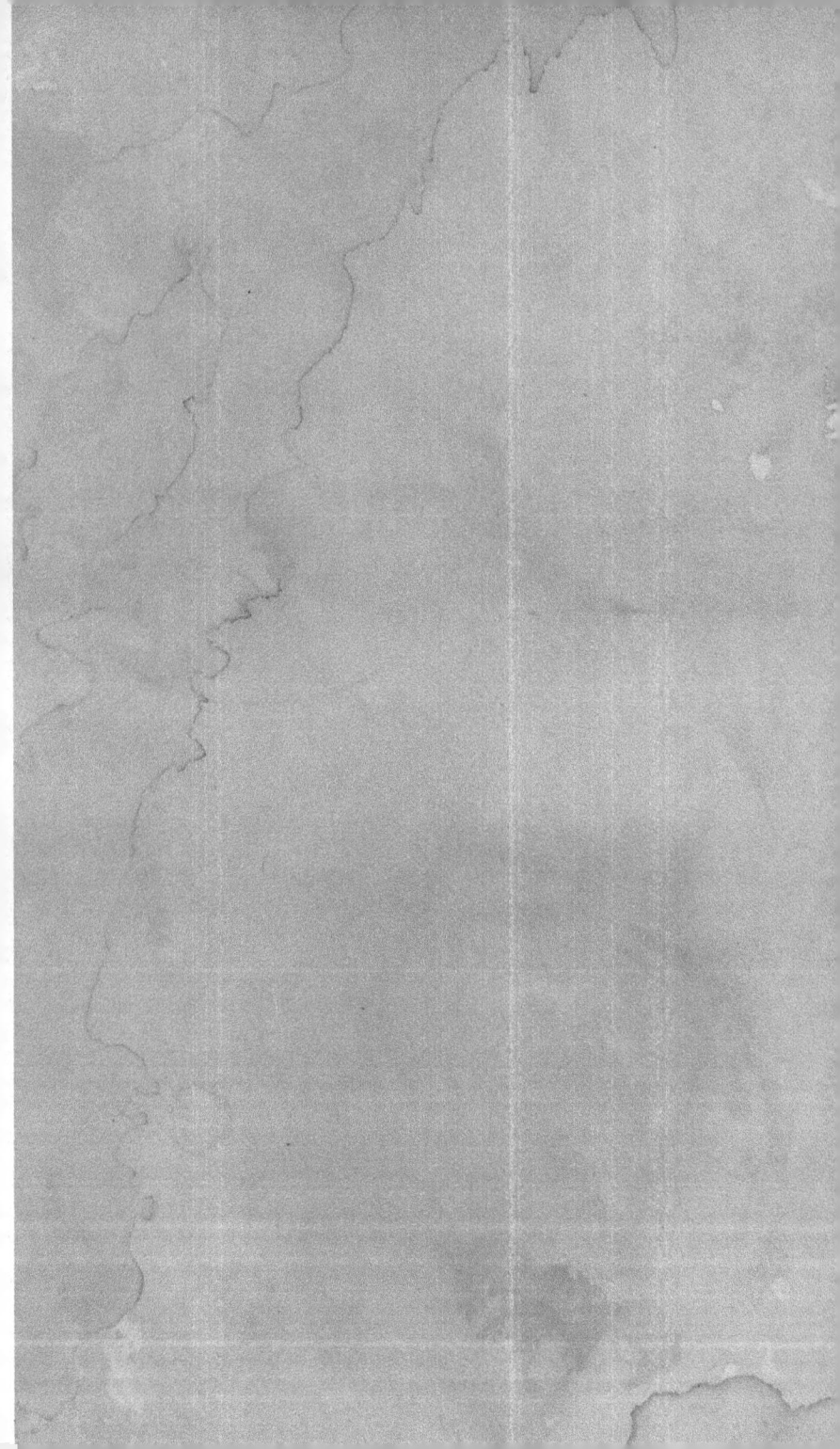

About the Author

Allister Nelson (she/her) is a multiple Pushcart Prize-nominated author whose work has appeared in The British Fantasy Society, Apex Magazine, ILLUMEN, Eternal Haunted Summer, Renewable Energy World, Frontiers in Health Communication, The National Science Foundation, Luna Station Quarterly, Prismatica Press, Coffin Bell, FunDead Publications, and many other venues. Her work has been translated internationally into Polish and Spanish, and has appeared in anthologies alongside Graham Masterston, Bill Willingham, Jane Yolen, and Alan Dean Foster. By day, she's a D.C.-adjacent Communications and Marketing Nut ("Allie's a Natural Washingtonian: a mile wide and an inch deep"), proud staff writer at Pride With a Bite, and senior technical and science writer. By night, she dabbles in prose, poems, Greco-Roman found feminism graphic novels, and illustrations. In her spare time, Allie is a wanderer of graveyards, weaver of fables, caster of literary aspersions, and gazer at alien starships. She'd like to kiss Mothman one day.